PLAYING
SOLITAIRE

PLAYING
SOLITAIRE

BY
NANCY ANTLE

DIAL BOOKS  NEW YORK

Published by Dial Books
A division of Penguin Putnam Inc.
345 Hudson Street
New York, New York 10014

Printed in the U.S.A. on acid-free paper

1 3 5 7 9 10 8 6 4 2

Library of Congress Cataloging in Publication Data
Antle, Nancy.
Playing solitaire/Nancy Antle.
p.   cm.
Summary: Living with her grandfather in
a small Oklahoma town, fourteen-year-old Ellie
is in constant fear that she will be approached
by her father, who is running from the police.
ISBN 0-8037-2406-3
[1. Fathers and daughters—Fiction.
2. Child abuse—Fiction. 3. Fugitives from justice—Fiction.
4. Grandfathers—Fiction. 5. Oklahoma—Fiction.] I. Title.
PZ7.A6294Pl   2000
[Fic]—dc21   99-30704   CIP

For my daughter, Liz, who changed the direction
of this book with her insightful comments

CHAPTER ONE

I don't know many things about my future. Not for sure. I don't know if I ever did. Lord knows, when I was living with Daddy, I sometimes wondered if I even had a future.

I know I miss Mama. I think about her when I wake up in the morning and when I go to bed at night. I guess I miss her most all of the time. Grandpa says he does too.

Mama was Grandpa's daughter, his only child. The two of us used to drive to Grandpa's every Sunday for as long as I can remember. Daddy went only a couple of times, but it was just as well. Grandpa made it real clear he didn't like him.

On our visits we'd go see Grandma in the nursing home too. She's been there for ten years—since I was four. There was a bad car accident and Grandpa was driving, but that's about all anybody ever told me.

Grandpa never came to our house much on account of Daddy. He really hated to be around him. But at the end, when Mama was in the hospital, Grandpa didn't let Daddy get in his way. He spent every day by Mama's bed.

One thing I know about my future is I have to start ninth grade—high school—at the end of the summer and I'm downright terrified. Right now it's still about four weeks off, and that's far enough that some days I can almost put it out of my mind. But sooner or later that awful thought comes creeping back.

Joy, Grandpa's next-door neighbor and best friend, said to me, "Ellie, with what you've survived so far, you can survive ninth grade."

I know she's right, and it isn't exactly like I don't know how to make friends. I didn't have that many, but heck, me and Janie Gann had been thick since kindergarten. For a while I even had a boyfriend named Chet, who taught me how to kiss. He said I was the prettiest thing he'd ever laid eyes on, though I reckon he hadn't been any farther than the Tulsa County line. 'Course, neither of them would be at my new school.

But even though I dreaded high school in Drasco, I figured the first day of ninth grade had to be better than the first day of seventh grade. Mama went and bought me a nice dress at the Goodwill store. She was so excited about it, I couldn't disappoint her and not wear it. So I did and I was the only girl all dolled up. Everyone kept gawking at me. Finally, right before the bell rang for first period, Ethelene walked up to me. She came real close and stared at my getup for a long time.

"I knew it," she said. "That dress was mine. I can just see where I spilled cherry punch on it at Alice Fae's wedding."

I wanted to crawl in a hole and die. I wished that God would come down and take me right then and there.

The only good thing about Drasco High is that Ethelene won't be there, and nobody knows what happened to me back in seventh grade.

Still, the kids might stare—thanks to Daddy. But I plan to stick to myself. I don't want to make friends just to lose them later on. It just about killed me to say good-bye to Janie and Chet. Neither one of them has written or anything. So I figure on getting through the next four years without anyone even noticing me.

Drasco is a new start for me. Nobody'll be feeling sorry for me 'cause my daddy was a mean drunk or 'cause Mama died of brain cancer. No one knows anything about Mama or Daddy—except what they remember from when Mama lived here. I aim to make it so they won't know about me or what Daddy did either. I'm going to be just an ordinary kid living with my ordinary grandpa. No one's going to mess that up. Not anyone.

I'm for sure going to play a lot of solitaire again. I already started. There's nothing in the world that I love more—all those cards in neat little rows always make me feel better. I do my best thinking when I play solitaire. When I first started playing, it was a great way to ignore Daddy. For a long time, before he decided we had to play cards *together*, if I had a game going he usually left me alone. Grandpa is another story.

After I moved in with him, it seemed like every time I'd sit down at the kitchen table with my worn-out deck of Bicycle cards, there was Grandpa. Oh, he'd act like he'd only come to the kitchen for a Coke or to pop him some popcorn, but I knew he was looking at me.

I could feel him getting all twitchy while he watched me try to shuffle the cards. I hated that.

I've had a hard time ever since the incident with Daddy. I'd always been great at shuffling—"Just like an old-time riverboat gambler," Mama used to say. Whenever I started to play, Grandpa would hover and act like any moment he was going to say, "Ellie, let me do that for you," or worse, suggest a round of gin.

Now, I don't have anything against gin—the card game, that is. It looks like fun sometimes when Grandpa and Joy play. I just don't like playing cards with other people. When I first got here, they were always asking me to join them, but they've quit asking now. Just as well. Grandpa gets ticked off at Joy when she beats him.

In the winter, when Mama first took sick, before she got really bad, we used to play solitaire side by side at the kitchen table. But we weren't playing together. We were just *being* together. We never talked much, just sat and sipped Cokes and ate Nutter Butter cookies, and dealt round after round of solitaire. Daddy didn't like it. I reckon he felt left out. So he got us to start playing poker with him. Five-card stud.

At first it was kind of fun—friendly little games after school. Then it was nickel games, and finally he was demanding I put up my baby-sitting money and Mama the tips she made at Buck's. Mama and I still sipped Cokes, but Daddy started slugging back great swallows of Jack Daniel's and cutting himself big slabs of Velveeta with his hunting knife. "It keeps me from getting drunk," he'd say about the cheese. But, of course, it didn't.

So whenever Grandpa was in the room while I was trying to play, I pretended he wasn't there. I knew that if I looked at him or spoke to him or gave him any kind of encouragement at all, he'd just grab the cards from my hand, shuffle them, and deal them out for me.

But Grandpa has to learn that I don't need his help. I can take care of myself—just like I always have.

And if Daddy ever gets within sight of me again, I'm going to kill him.

CHAPTER

TWO

I can't remember a time when I didn't know Joy Collins. Seems like she's always lived next door to Grandma and Grandpa. Joy is the only person I know who has been married and divorced three times. Mama told me once that Joy had been Grandpa's high-school sweetheart before he joined the Army. I always wondered how Grandma felt about having Joy live right next door.

Joy was kind of like having another grandma. She treated me like kin—meaning she didn't think twice about yelling at me or hugging me. She was always giving advice too. One Thursday Grandpa and I helped her carry in some things she'd picked up at the store—mostly cat food and toilet paper.

"You know," Joy said. "I always found comfort in a dog. That's what you need, Ellie. A dog."

"But you don't have a dog," I said.

I dropped a heavy bag on the counter as Siam, Joy's black cat, wound its way between my ankles.

"I haven't been able to bring myself to get another dog since old Duke died last month. But I usually have a dog. Don't I, Tom?"

Grandpa grinned at her. "Yeah, and you usually have a husband. Next thing you'll be suggesting that Ellie get married."

Joy glared at Grandpa and slammed a cabinet door.

"No chance of that," I said. "I'm never getting married."

"Now, don't let one bad experience turn you against the idea," Grandpa said. I knew he was referring to Mama and Daddy.

"Oh, I'm not against marriage," I said. "I just want to live by myself."

"Very sensible," Joy said, glaring at Grandpa again. "I think it's time more of us women quit thinking we have to find Prince Charming before we can live happily ever after."

"No such thing anyway," Grandpa said. "Just happy some of the time and waiting to be happy the rest of the time."

"I think I'll like living on my own," I said.

"What do you think of that, Joy? She's only been here a month and she's already making plans to leave. Just when I was getting used to sharing the bathroom with her."

Grandpa put his arm around me and squeezed my shoulders.

"Come off it, Grandpa," I said. "You liked having the house to yourself."

I pretended not to notice the look that passed between Joy and Grandpa. They were always doing that when I was around, as if I were too dumb to notice. They started with the looks as soon as Joy brought Grandpa to get me with my hand all bandaged up at the hospital. Then they took me to the police station. Grandpa had to sign some papers, and everything had to be dredged up all over again. Daddy and the poker playing, Daddy and his hunting knife, and had Daddy ever hit Mama before she died, and on and on.

The worried looks from Joy and Grandpa just flew around the room that day. Even the sheriff got in on it. I didn't want their looks. I *knew* I was going to be okay. Why couldn't they see that?

Grandpa cleared his throat. I thought he was going to say he liked having me around or something. But he didn't. He just squeezed my shoulders again. I swallowed a sudden lump in my throat. What the heck was wrong with me?

Joy looked at her watch. "Hellfire and damnation. We've missed ten minutes of our soap, Tom."

"Heaven forbid," Grandpa said, and winked at me. Joy took some money out of her wallet. Grandpa walked into the living room and turned on the TV.

We'd been through the same routine every day since I got there. Joy would pick up Grandpa at the Shell station, and the two of them would rush home for lunch and to watch their soaps on TV. Most days they picked up lunch on the way home, but if they got hung up at work, they'd ask me to walk to the Dairy Deal. Joy couldn't stand to miss her program.

"Ellie, get us some burgers," Joy said, handing me the money. "Get whatever you want too. You want a milk shake, Tom?"

"Yes, please," Grandpa shouted from the living room.

"I don't," she said. "My doctor said I need to lose twenty-five pounds." She rolled her eyes. "Like that's gonna happen."

I walked out into the bright sunshine and Joy's front yard. I started to sweat before I'd even walked half a block. But I didn't mind going to get lunch. I secretly hoped to spot a certain cute guy named Dex I'd seen from the front porch every day. I knew his name 'cause his friends were always calling out to him from their bikes.

"Hey, Dex. Let's go fishing."

"Dex, you tired yet? Let's go eat."

Dex always seemed to be wearing an Oklahoma State University cap over his blond hair. He had deep dimples that he'd flashed at me a couple of times as he zipped up or down the street. I'd barely smiled back and never been brave enough to say anything to him. Actually, I had no intention of having anything to do with him. But I figured it couldn't hurt to look.

The thing that worried me about the Dairy Deal was the possibility that a whole mess of kids my age would be there when I went. I really worried, especially in the beginning, when my hand was still bandaged. Problem was, there wasn't much else to do in Drasco in the summer besides hang out drinking slushies and playing video games at the Dairy Deal.

It always seemed to me when I walked in that the noise died down and everyone looked at me. Kind of like in those old Western movies when some new guy in town walked into a saloon. Maybe it was my imagination.

But Daddy's picture had been in the paper saying he was wanted by the police, and there was an article about what he'd done. In full detail. At least the paper didn't give my name. Just in case, I'd asked Grandpa if I could go by his last name. He agreed without even asking questions. I was now Ellie Whiteday instead of Ellie McCoy. So I was pretty sure no one would figure anything out. But I still worried about it.

When I got to the Dairy Deal, I shoved my left hand into the pocket of my jeans. Dex, in his usual cap, was sitting on his bike and reaching down to pet a dog lying in front of the door. My heart raced and my hands started sweating. And then he just straightened up and took off. He smiled at me over his shoulder and waved. Before I could think, I waved back, but he had turned away by then and didn't see.

I looked inside the shop and was relieved to see only a couple of kids. Both looked younger than me. The dog still lay right across the doorway.

It was a mutt—a cross between a beagle and something else—hard to tell what. It had big brown eyes, no collar, and a funny little half tail that must've gotten cut off somehow. When I first saw that tail, a dark memory uncoiled inside of me like a snake and I felt sick. The feeling passed as soon as I breathed deep and pushed that snake back down. The dog thumped its tail as I stepped over it.

For a few brief seconds that dog—and I hope Mama forgives me for this—reminded me of Mama. I think it was the big eyes and the friendly way the dog thumped its pathetic tail. I patted it a few times on the head and rubbed its back on my way inside.

"Your dog?" I asked Ruth, the owner of the Dairy Deal.

"No. It's a stray," she said. "Been hanging around here begging for leftovers. Comes off and on."

While I waited for my order, I turned to look back. The dog stood up and started wiggling all over, wagging its stumpy tail when it saw me looking. I figured it knew by now that most people went inside empty-handed and came outside with food. Pretty smart dog.

I got my order and left. The dog sat down the moment I walked through the door—just as if I had told it to sit. It put up its right paw to shake. I don't know if it was that, or those deep brown Mama eyes, or its stumpy tail, or just the fact that Joy put the idea into my head, but that was the moment I got myself a dog.

C H A P T E R

T
H
R
E
E

By the time I got the burgers home, I had discovered I had a girl dog. I named her Birdie—partly because she had the face of a bird dog that used to hang around my old house. And Birdie was Mama's middle name.

Grandpa and Joy seemed happy that I'd gotten myself a dog. Grandpa especially liked the name. He gave me money to get dog food, a leash and a collar, and some flea shampoo. Joy said she'd take Birdie to the vet later for her shots.

After I came back from the store, I gave Birdie a bath

and showed her my room, with the braid rug where she could sleep, and the backyard, where she could bury bones or do whatever else a dog might want to do.

I figured having a dog for a friend was way better than having a person. I could count on her not asking me any hard questions.

Grandpa lived on the far north side of town, so his backyard edged right up to some scrubby-looking woods that probably went all the way to Strang or Spavinaw with few houses in between. A good place for me and Birdie to go for walks and explore.

While we were outside that first day, a brown-and-black German shepherd mix with a white chest came out of the woods and headed right over to Birdie. The dog was pretty skinny but it had on a collar and tags. His eyes didn't look friendly enough for me to try and pet him.

When Birdie saw the shepherd, she wagged her tail and rolled over on her back to show her belly. Then she jumped up and wiggled all over while they smelled each other. They ran around the yard a few times together, wrestling and barking. Finally the shepherd ran back into the woods. He stopped and turned around once like he was waiting for Birdie to follow him, but she sat down on my foot and didn't budge. Birdie whimpered a little.

Later Birdie and I took a walk over to Lake Chouteau. I skipped a few rocks, something Mama had taught me, and threw a stick for Birdie. She was good at getting it but not at bringing it back. She would just lie down and start chewing on it as though it were the best present she had ever had.

I hoped that Dex would notice that I'd adopted the dog he'd been petting. But we didn't run into him.

When Birdie and I got back home, I realized I hadn't thought about Daddy or high school all day. 'Course, I had thought about Mama, but it hadn't been in a sad way. Not really. I'd thought about how much she would have liked Birdie. I reckoned Joy was right about a dog being a comfort.

As usual the good stuff, like Birdie, didn't happen to me without some bad coming along. Mama used to say that if God didn't send the terrible times, we'd never appreciate the great ones. Which I guess was one way of looking at it. But it always seemed like what went wrong in other people's lives—F's on math tests and cars breaking down—wasn't quite the same sort of thing that went wrong in mine.

A few days after I got Birdie, Joy came over to eat supper with us. Grandpa walked home early and started in fixing fried chicken, mashed potatoes, biscuits, gravy, and green beans. When I lived with Mama and Daddy, I mostly ate peanut butter sandwiches. Sometimes Buck, the owner of the café where Mama worked, would give me a free chicken-fried steak for supper. I always loved that. But I don't know how to cook. Grandpa is a good cook. Though he isn't exactly patient enough to let me try to do anything except peel potatoes. I don't mind.

That evening we ate on TV trays in the living room while Joy and Grandpa watched an infomercial about how they could get rich selling Nature Slim.

"If we decide to sell this, Tom," Joy said, "I'll have to be our first customer." She took a bite of chicken and sighed.

"Joy, you know you look just fine," Grandpa said. "Doesn't she, Ellie?"

I nodded. I supposed that she was a little plump, but as far as I was concerned, she was exactly like someone named Joy who owned a flower shop should be.

Just when the super-thin person on the set was telling us how she lost more than a hundred pounds with Nature Slim, the phone rang.

"Get that, would you, Ellie?" Grandpa said. "If it's Ned calling to nag me about joining his bowling team again, tell him I'm not here."

I picked up the phone on the third ring. Birdie followed me into the kitchen and lay down on my feet.

"Hello?" I answered.

"Ellie?" a voice asked.

I'd read books where people said their blood ran cold. I always thought that was just talk—just some fancy way to say that they were really scared. But I swear when I heard that voice, that's exactly how I felt. A chill ran down my whole body and I started to shake.

"Ellie?" the voice said again. "It's Daddy."

C H A P T E R

F O U R

I hung up the phone without answering. Then I sat down on the kitchen floor and hugged Birdie. She squirmed and wiggled and licked my face. Even that didn't make the moment feel real. I felt like I was underwater, moving slowly, without sound, and everything was blurry around the edges.

Grandpa and Joy came into the kitchen carrying their supper dishes.

"Who was on the phone?" Grandpa asked.

"Wrong number," I said hoarsely, then coughed. My voice sounded too normal in my ears.

I didn't like the idea of saying "Daddy" out loud. It meant somehow that he'd broken into my new life. I wasn't going to let him mess this one up too.

Other than that I didn't have one good reason not to tell Grandpa who was on the phone. He'd never given me any reason to think he wouldn't help me if I needed it. I suppose I was just used to taking care of myself—handling my own problems. I also knew that Grandpa wouldn't exactly approve of how I planned to take care of Daddy.

The police had been looking for Daddy for two months. I didn't figure they were looking too hard—after all, he hadn't killed me. And I knew that he would try to see me sometime, but I hadn't figured that he'd call first.

Finally I got up. The chill was gone, but my hands still shook when I took the plates from the counter and started scraping the chicken bones into the trash.

"Here," Joy said. She had my plate of food and glass of tea from the living room. She put it on the kitchen table. "Better finish your supper. We'll clean up."

"I'm not very hungry."

"Hey," Grandpa said. "Don't you like my famous fried chicken?"

"It's great," I said. I tried to smile. "I'm just not too hungry tonight."

"You probably got worn out peeling all those potatoes," Joy teased. "I'll put your plate in the refrigerator. You can eat it later if you get hungry."

"If I don't beat you to it," Grandpa said.

"You leave her chicken alone," Joy warned.

She filled the sink with soapy water and started washing the dishes, rinsing them, and putting them in the rack to drip. Grandpa took a clean dish towel from the drawer and started drying.

I picked up my pack of cards and my glass of iced tea.

"I'm going to sit out front," I said. The sun was sinking behind the trees and it would be dark soon, but I needed some room to think. "C'mon, Birdie."

I hesitated at the screen door and took a deep breath. Daddy could be anywhere. He could be in California working or he could be down at the Dairy Deal getting a slushy with the evening crowd.

I walked over to the end table next to Grandpa's recliner and opened the drawer. Grandpa's gun was still there—heavy and dark, right next to the *TV Guide*. Joy had insisted he keep it unloaded since Grandma sometimes wandered home, and you could never tell what she might do. He kept the bullets in a little box in the top of the hall closet just a few steps away.

It wouldn't take me long to load it if I needed to.

I practiced one day—timing myself. Thirty-two seconds. Mama taught me to shoot one summer when Daddy was away on a job. The gun was so heavy, I had always needed two hands to fire it. But I was pretty sure I could do it with one hand now, if I had to.

I closed the drawer and walked out onto the porch. The tall hedges that surrounded Grandpa's yard made dark shadows over the lawn and porch but the sky through the leaves was still pink. I sat on the top step and dealt out the cards next to me. Birdie lay in the grass and panted.

I missed Mama more than ever right then. I wanted her to put her arms around me and tell me how it was going to be when I was all grown up and out on my own. When I was living happily ever after.

When she was alive, Daddy was mostly gone, working construction just like Grandpa until Grandpa injured his back and bought the Shell station. In fact, Grandpa introduced Daddy to Mama. I always imagined that he thought that was just about the sorriest thing he ever did.

Anyway, when Daddy was gone, Mama and I were always pretty happy. She had to work long hours in the café some days, but Buck always gave me free Cokes and let me sit in a booth at the back while I did my homework. Sometimes when Daddy was home, it was okay. But whenever he started in drinking, he'd get mean—"verbally abusive" was what the social worker who visited me in the hospital called it. I thought that made it not sound bad enough. Daddy would go on and on about how much trouble we were and how he should just kill us so we wouldn't bother him anymore. He'd accuse Mama of sleeping with other men and tell me I was ugly and stupid.

He probably only ever hit Mama or me once or twice, but when he drank, he seemed so crazy that I was always expecting something awful to happen. Even when he was being nice, I would wonder how long it was going to last.

Daddy stayed sober for almost a year once. That was probably the best year of my life. I must have been twelve, almost thirteen, 'cause right after that we found out that Mama had brain cancer, and Daddy started in drinking right away. Mama said it was because he was sad.

Mama tried to change Daddy every way she knew how except leaving him. I never understood why she didn't do that. I always hoped she would.

I swallowed the tightness in my throat and dealt out another round of solitaire. Just when I'd laid the last card on the porch, Birdie jumped up and barked. I listened, trying to hear what she'd heard. The chill returned.

"Birdie, come here." She came and sat beside me on the porch. Her stubby tail barely wagged, as if she wasn't sure whether or not to be happy about the sound of footsteps we could hear coming up the road in the fading light.

CHAPTER

FIVE

"Inside, Birdie," I said. I jumped up and held the screen door open for her while I stood inside the living room. She thumped her tail on the step and looked at me over her shoulder. She didn't want to come in. She wanted to make friends with whoever was coming.

"Birdie. Come," I said firmly and held the door wider. She wiggled down to the bottom step and sat, waiting.

I gave up and closed the screen door. My heart was racing just like it did in the middle of the night when I dreamed about Daddy. I kept my eyes on the door and backed over to the table next to Grandpa's chair. And his gun.

"Hey, Ellie, wait up," a voice called. It sounded familiar, but it wasn't Daddy. I walked back to the screen door and looked out to see Dex grinning at me. I was so shocked he knew my name, I couldn't speak.

"Didn't mean to scare you," he said, coming up onto the porch. "I just thought I'd visit since we're neighbors and all." He looked down at his feet and then back at me. He took his cap off and ran his fingers through his hair. "I mean, I've been seeing you for weeks, but we've never talked or anything."

"Oh," I said. While I tried to think of what else to say, Birdie bumped his leg with her wet nose and held up her paw to shake.

"Hey, this is the dog that's been hanging out at the Dairy Deal." He reached down to pat her head and grinned at me again. I nodded. "How'd you teach him to shake hands?"

"Her," I said. "And I didn't. She taught me."

"What's her name?"

"Birdie." I walked out onto the porch, thinking that

would seem more sociable. I didn't want him to think I didn't want to talk to him. But Lord, I was having trouble breathing and thinking, let alone coming up with anything interesting to say. I sat down on the top step and Dex sat down next to me.

"I'm glad you took her," he said. "She needed someone."

For some reason I remembered the German shepherd who had come to welcome Birdie her first day at our house.

"You wouldn't happen to know a dog that looks like a German shepherd mix—black and brown with a white front?"

"Might be my dog—depending on what he did," he said. "Did he turn over your grandpa's trash cans or eat Joy's cat?"

I laughed. "No. He just came to play."

"You should feel honored. Old Jake doesn't usually take to strange dogs."

Birdie put up her paw again to shake.

"Mom said you were going into the ninth grade like me," Dex said.

I nodded, feeling uneasy. I wondered what else he knew about me.

"She said we even played together once when we

were four or five—when you and your mom were visiting. Least that's what she told me."

I frowned at him, trying to remember.

"Don't worry," he said. "I don't remember it either."

But somewhere in the back of my mind I sort of remembered a long day at Grandpa's house with a blond-haired boy.

There was an awkward silence while Dex and I both petted Birdie, who looked like she was in ecstasy. I shoved my other hand under my leg and felt the smooth wood of the porch.

"Where do you live?" I finally said, in a hurry to fill the silence.

"Just up the street," he answered, like he was in a hurry too.

He looked down at my cards then, all laid out for a game.

"You like to play cards?" he asked.

"Just solitaire."

"Great," he said. "I know this neat game of solitaire for two called Hell. I can never find anyone who likes to play, though. We could play together. I'll come over sometime and show you."

"I don't really like . . ." I started to say. But before I could add "playing cards," a woman's voice hollered, "DEEEX-TERRRR!"

"I gotta go," he said. "See you soon. You too, Birdie." Birdie thumped her tail beside me and we watched him run down the sidewalk. I smiled to myself as the sound of his footsteps faded up the street.

CHAPTER

SIX

When Joy took me and Birdie to the vet, we found out Birdie was pregnant. I wondered who the father was, then whispered to her that she was better off without him and that I'd take good care of her.

I didn't think Grandpa would like the idea too much, but he just laughed when I told him—said puppies ought to keep me pretty busy for a while.

That night when I was lying in bed with Birdie on the floor next to me, I reached down and felt her belly. Mama told me once that when she was pregnant with me, I always started kicking whenever she wanted to go to sleep. I wondered if puppies might do the same thing.

I kept my hand on her side for a long time while it rose and fell. Finally I felt something move and then another something. It made me smile to myself in the darkness. I hoped Dex would come over soon so I could tell him about the puppies.

You'd think that falling asleep thinking about cute little puppies and a cute boy, I'd have happy dreams. But even if I managed not to think about Daddy all day, he always made an appearance at night. This night was no different.

I did dream about puppies at first, wiggling and whining. Then suddenly Daddy was standing in the middle of them. He had a big bag and he started putting the puppies into the bag, saying we couldn't take care of them. I wanted to stop him but I couldn't move. When I tried to talk to him, my mouth felt like it was full of cotton and the words wouldn't come out. The puppies yelped and then started crying. They sounded like real babies. The crying turned to wailing. . . . Then Birdie barked and I woke up, my heart racing as usual.

Birdie barked again, and I realized that noise was

coming from underneath my bedroom floor. There was a long low guttural moan followed by a hiss. Cats. Birdie whimpered and paced.

I heard Grandpa get up in the next room, cursing. He stood in the doorway to my room, holding a broom.

"I swear I'm going to strangle that cat!" He pounded the broom handle on top of my floor a few times, but that only seemed to make the cats madder. "Hell's bells," he said, and tromped down the hallway. I got up and padded after him.

Grandpa slammed out the front door and hooked up the hose to the faucet at the corner of the house.

"Turn on the water when I tell you," he said to me. I watched him walk down the driveway. Joy came scurrying out her back door holding a flashlight and pulling on her bathrobe.

"That must be Siam getting in a fight again," she said. "I hope he's okay. Don't you hurt him now, Tom."

"I'm going to throttle him when I get a chance," Grandpa said. "Waking me up at all hours."

"Well, if you'd fix that damn hole in the side of your house, the cats couldn't get under there," she said.

"If you'd keep your damn cat in the house at night, he wouldn't be getting into fights under my house!"

The first time I'd heard them argue like that I'd been worried, but I finally figured out it didn't mean anything. It wasn't like when Mama and Daddy fought. For one thing, Joy argued back.

"Turn it on," Grandpa hollered to me.

I twisted the faucet, then joined Grandpa and Joy by the hole in the crawl space. Grandpa crouched down and sprayed water under the house while Joy shined the flashlight into the darkness.

"Do you see them?" she asked.

Grandpa shook his head and kept moving the hose through the opening. Pretty soon we were all standing in a puddle of water. Grandpa pointed the hose at the ground and peered inside.

"I don't see them," he said. "Ellie, turn off the water. Maybe I'll be able to hear them."

Just as I turned to go, there was a loud, angry meow from under the house, and two wet cats came shooting out of the hole. Neither one of them was Siam. Grandpa was off balance, and they knocked him over in the process. He landed with a splat on his butt right in the middle of the water. The hose still spewed water around him.

"Perfect," he said.

I ran to turn off the faucet. By the time I came back, Joy was sitting in the puddle with Grandpa and they were laughing hysterically. Just watching them made me laugh too.

"And it wasn't even Siam," Joy finally said, catching her breath.

"Guess I'll nail a couple boards over that hole one of these days," Grandpa said.

Joy got up, then we each took one of Grandpa's hands and pulled him up. "But not tonight," she said. "I need some sleep."

"Me too," Grandpa said.

"Me three," I said.

"Y'all want a piece of chocolate cake first?" Joy asked.

"Chocolate cake?" Grandpa said. "You didn't tell me you baked. You've been holding out on me."

"I don't have to tell you everything. Besides, I made it for Ellie."

I laughed some more as I followed the two of them, arguing again, into Joy's comfortable kitchen for cake and milk.

CHAPTER

SEVEN

While I was washing the breakfast dishes a few mornings later, the phone rang. It startled me so much, I dropped a soapy glass on the kitchen floor and watched it shatter.

It was a Saturday and Joy had gone to work early. I could see her empty driveway from the kitchen window. Grandpa had gone to visit Grandma at the nursing home. I had decided not to go with him.

The phone kept ringing. Birdie stood on the back porch step and barked through the screen. I stared at the phone, waiting for it to stop. Finally it did.

At that moment the only possible person I could come up with for who would call was Daddy. It had been more than a week since Dex had stopped by, and I'd given up on him calling or coming back. I knew that Grandpa had friends who phoned all the time. But I was still having Daddy dreams, and the only thing my fear would let me believe was that it was him on the other end of the line. Just like it had been before.

I went to get the broom from the hall closet. Just as the last of the glass was swept into the dustpan, the phone rang again. This time it stopped after only three rings.

I let Birdie in the back and locked the screen door, then closed and dead-bolted the wooden one too. I walked to the living room and did the same to the front door. Sitting in Grandpa's recliner, I opened the drawer of the end table and stared at the gun for a long time—waiting—wondering if I should load it. Finally Birdie bumped her nose into my arm, asking me to pet her and waking me up.

"Good girl," I said, and patted her head. I closed the drawer slowly.

Birdie stood up suddenly and barked facing the front door. I heard footsteps on the porch and took a deep breath. It's just the mailman, I told myself.

The person on the porch knocked at the door. A face peered through the window screen. I could just see the outline of a head and a familiar cap through the sheer curtains.

"Ellie, you in there?" It was Dex.

I'd been ready to kill Daddy if it had been him on the porch. Dex about gave me a heart attack. 'Course, it wasn't exactly his fault—he didn't know what was going on. Birdie barked again and her tail looked like a deformed windmill on high speed as I unlocked the front door and the screen.

"I knew you were home," Dex said. "How come you didn't answer the phone?"

"I . . . I was out back with Birdie," I stumbled over my lie. I wished I could just talk to him like a normal person.

"I brought my cards," he said. He held up an un-opened deck of cards still with the little sticker over the end of the box.

"I don't really want to play cards right now," I said.

"Aw, come on, please?" He smiled his gorgeous smile at me.

"Well, maybe . . ." I said.

"I knew you wouldn't let me down." He followed me into the kitchen, where I let Birdie out again. "Get your cards. We need two decks to play Hell."

"Let's play at the table," I said. "It'll be better." I was also thinking it would be a good way to hide things.

He sat down in one of the chairs. "You got any iced tea?"

"Next you'll be wanting lunch to go with it," I said before I thought. It was the way Joy talked to Grandpa or the way I used to talk to Janie, but I didn't know what he'd think. When he laughed, I was relieved.

I took down two glasses from the cabinet and poured tea into them from the pitcher in the refrigerator. He sat at the table and shuffled his cards three or four times, then dealt them out.

"That looks like regular old solitaire to me," I said. I stood next to him at the table.

"It is," he said. "Deal your cards out too. I'll show you what to do."

I sat down opposite him and did as he said. I skipped over the shuffling part and dealt them out slowly and carefully. He didn't seem to notice anything. He was mostly in a hurry to get on with the game.

"It's real easy," he said. "We just go along playing regular solitaire, putting our aces in the usual place. But—and this is the part that makes it interesting— we can play off of each other's cards. The first one to get all their cards up on the aces wins. Oh, and when you put your last card up there you shout, 'HELL!'"

I nodded. I was just going to concentrate on getting through the game. Dex tapped his foot on the floor like he couldn't wait to win.

"Ready, GO!" he said all at once.

I started turning over cards three at a time. First up was an ace of diamonds. I put it above my row of cards. But before I could put my two of diamonds on top of it, Dex slapped his down.

"Gotcha!" he said.

I returned the favor when I put my five of clubs on his four before he could use his five.

"Gotcha back," I said.

The game rushed on like that for quite a while until he finally shouted, "HELL!" as he threw his last card down.

Sweat trickled down the sides of his face, and he took a big swallow of tea. For a minute some snaky memories uncurled in my head, but I pushed them down again. Playing Hell with this boy was nothing like playing poker with Daddy, I told myself. It was almost fun. It would have been more fun but I had to start shuffling or he'd have noticed when I dealt them out that they were coming up in order. I shuffled them on my lap. It was hard and I worried that they'd all end up on the floor.

"Best out of three?" Dex asked.

"Sure," I said. "Why not? Do you want some more tea?"

He nodded and then started dealing out his cards again. I poured him more tea and plunked a few cubes of ice into the glass too.

The table was a big help, just as I had hoped. I shuffled my cards down on my lap where Dex couldn't see. He didn't act like he thought I was trying to cheat or anything.

We ended up playing most of the day, though we did stop at lunchtime to go to the Dairy Deal and eat. The place was packed with kids, and Dex introduced me to a bunch of his friends. They were all polite and said they were glad to know me. I figured that was because I was with Dex, but I didn't care.

I ate lunch right there in front of everyone, and no one seemed to notice a thing. I must have been getting really good at hiding what Daddy did. I even started to think I might actually like going to school.

Dex turned down an invitation from one of his friends to go swimming out at Jensen's Dock after lunch.

"Nah," he said. "Me and Ellie got plans." I felt my face get hot, but there was no doubt that was one of the good moments God sent me. We went back to Grandpa's house.

Cards with Dex was a lot like playing with Mama. We didn't talk all that much, but it felt like a comfortable silence now.

'Course, we did talk some. I found out he loved the ice cream at the Dairy Deal, and he'd just read *The Outsiders* by S. E. Hinton (we were both supposed to read it before school started) and decided it was the best book he'd ever read. Or actually, heard. His mom had read it to him.

"You might as well know right off that I have learning problems," he said. "Everyone at school will tell you soon enough. I still have trouble reading and have to have a special tutor. I don't like to talk much about it, though. It's just something you should know if we're going to be friends."

I felt a rush of happiness when he said "friends," but wasn't sure what else to say. I mumbled something back like "Thanks for telling me" and then changed the subject. I told him *The Outsiders* was my new favorite book too. Which it was, and S. E. Hinton living in Tulsa made it extra special.

About four o'clock his mom called and asked him to go to the store to pick up some stuff for supper.

"One last game, okay?" he said after he hung up.

I nodded and laid out my cards.

"Go!" I yelled as soon as he'd dealt his last card.

"Hey," he said. "No fair." He laughed, though.

Some games nothing much had happened. Once in a while we'd even played a round where neither one of us won. But this one was really fast. We kept turning over cards, racing each other to put our cards on the aces.

I could see that Dex was going to win. He was using two hands to move his cards up. I was using only my right hand. But I was pretty fast. Then it happened. I got carried away and started using my left hand too. I kept it clenched slightly, and moved the cards a little awkwardly. Still, I thought it looked pretty ordinary. It made me a lot faster, and to tell the truth, I was so involved in the game, I didn't think about Dex seeing anything.

We kept slapping cards down as fast as we could. Finally I grabbed my last card with my left hand and slammed it down on the table.

"Hell!" I shouted. It was one of the few games I'd won all day, and I was pretty proud of myself. I smiled at Dex, but the look on his face said it all. He was staring down at my left hand, which I had put out in the open for the whole world to see right on top of the king of diamonds.

He hadn't taken his eyes off my left hand in the long moments since I'd shouted "Hell" either. He was the first person to look at my hand since Grandpa and Joy had seen it at the hospital—the left one that was missing part of three fingers right between the first and second knuckles. Right where Daddy had cut them off with his hunting knife on the last night that I was with him.

CHAPTER

EIGHT

I should have known better than to think that any good could come from playing cards with somebody. After the incident with Daddy, you'd think I'd have learned my lesson.

The silence that filled the room that day seemed to last forever. Dex started right away separating his cards from mine. I waited for him to ask about my fingers, but he didn't. It wasn't like he could've missed them.

When he was finished gathering his cards, he shoved them into his back pocket and got up to go.

"I'd better get to the store," he said. "Maybe we can

play again tomorrow after church." He looked at the floor instead of me when he said it.

"Okay," I answered, wondering if he'd show up. Did I hope he would or wouldn't? I guess I did like being around him.

If only I could see inside his head and know what he thought about me now. Did he think my hand was too creepy to be around?

When he was gone, I went to the back door to get Birdie so we could go for a walk. She wasn't there, but that wasn't unusual. When I first got my dog, she stayed with me every second while she got used to having a home. Now it seemed like she was always gallivanting off for walks in the woods or down to the lake.

I called her name before I left, but she didn't come. I walked up our block and turned right at Seminole Street, which ran along the north edge of Drasco between the town and the woods.

Walks were like playing solitaire. They were my other time to think. Lord knows I needed to sort things out. I didn't understand why Dex hadn't asked about my fingers. Everyone who had ever seen them asked. Which was why I'd tried to hide them so much. Who wanted to admit that her own father cut off her fingers?

I didn't walk on the road but trekked into the woods

about fifteen feet and followed along from there. I didn't like being out in the open where people in passing cars could see me. Never mind that about one car a day traveled by. That one could be Daddy.

There wasn't much along Seminole but a couple of little churches—the Free Will Baptist and the Pentecostal—and the nursing home where Grandma was.

I hadn't planned on visiting her until I found myself there. The home was only five minutes from Grandpa's. At the entrance Birdie came bounding out of the woods and barked at me. I reached down and rubbed behind her ears. She licked my hand. We walked up the concrete ramp to the front door. Birdie trotted inside ahead of me.

I always hated the smell of nursing homes—like rubbing alcohol and overcooked vegetables and pee all mixed together. Mama worked as a nurse's aide in one for a while when I was little. Sometimes she'd take me to visit the residents. The minute I walked in the door, everyone would come over to talk to me, to shake my hand and pat my head. It was kind of scary at first till I got used to it. They just wanted someone new to talk to—something different to take the sameness out of their day.

Grandma's nursing home was like the one Mama

had worked in, but the residents here knew me better since I'd visited so often.

As I walked across the lobby with Birdie, Mr. Chitwood, a white-haired man in a wheelchair, said, "Got yourself a dog, I see, young lady. Your grandma will like that."

I put my hand on his shoulder. He covered it with his own gnarled one.

"How's Grandma?" I asked.

"She was here this morning," he said. He tapped the side of his head and winked. "Couldn't get a word in edgewise." He chuckled. "Reckon she's completely worn out by now. Might be gone again."

"How are you doing?" I asked.

"Well, my arthritis is acting up," he said. "But I really can't complain." He patted Birdie. "Better go visit your grandma. We'll be eating supper shortly."

I nodded and headed to Grandma's room.

"Don't forget to stop by my room on your way out," Mr. Chitwood called after me.

"I won't," I said. Mama and I used to stop by his room every time we came to see Grandma. I kept visiting him even after Mama wasn't there to remind me.

For as long as I had known Mr. Chitwood, he'd been in a wheelchair. His hair had gotten whiter and his arthritis had bent his hands more, but other than that he hadn't changed much over the years.

Mr. Chitwood owned the Shell station before Grandpa. Everyone in Drasco knew Mr. Chitwood back then. Mama said he was always lending her a dollar's worth of gas for the beat-up old car she had when she was sixteen. When Mama died, Mr. Chitwood had been one of the first people to send me and Daddy a card and some flowers.

At the end of the hall Grandma's door was open. She was sitting in a chair facing the window. I was glad to see she wasn't tied down. Sometimes she got out of control and had to be restrained. Although it was always terrible to see, I understood why they had to do it. Once Mama and I came to see her when she was mad about something. She'd overturned her big hospital bed, tipped over her dresser, and thrown a chair across the room. It was surprising and a little scary that someone so small could be so strong.

On this day Grandma looked pretty calm. Opal, the head nurse, was beside her.

"Hi, Ellie," Opal said. "Your grandpa was telling us you had a dog now." She bent down and Birdie wiggled over to have her head scratched.

Grandma didn't move an inch. She took a deep breath, and a strand of her long, dark hair fell across her right eye. She wasn't nearly as old as most of the people in the nursing home. I figured she was about fifty-five or so. Mr. Chitwood was close to eighty.

The trouble with Grandma was her mind. The car wreck she and Grandpa had been in was pretty bad. Her head got bashed in, and for a while everybody thought she was going to die. Though she survived, nobody thought she'd be able to do anything. But she fooled them again and could do just about everything—most of the time. Trouble was, sometimes her mind just drifted away, and she didn't hear anybody talking to her or know exactly where she was. Even when her mind was working, she got confused, which I think is why she got so mad sometimes.

When she first went to stay at the nursing home, she used to get it into her head that Grandpa needed supper fixed. She'd walk home and Grandpa would find her in the kitchen. He said she'd always fix pretty interesting meals too—like Oreos and ice cream, or cheese and sardines on crackers. My kind of cooking.

She didn't wander home nearly so often now. Especially since Grandpa lit into the staff about paying more attention to her. But she did come home right after I moved in. Joy said she was probably just making sure I was okay. But I don't think she understands what happened—even though I told her.

Mama said once that Grandma's mind was kind of like a lamp with a short. Sometimes it worked and sometimes it didn't.

"So how's Grandma today?" I asked Opal.

"She was doing real well until about an hour ago. Talked a blue streak to your grandpa this morning. She seems to have drifted off on us now."

I walked over and put my hand on her shoulder.

"Hi, Grandma," I said softly.

She smiled for a brief moment.

"I'll bring you both a couple of Cokes," Opal said. "She always likes to have a little something with her guests."

The nurse hurried out. I stood in front of Grandma and she stared right at me. But she didn't move at all, which made me think she hadn't really seen me. Birdie put her head in Grandma's lap, and Grandma began stroking her head.

"Who are you?" Grandma suddenly asked.

"Ellie," I said. "Your granddaughter."

"Who?"

"Rachel's daughter."

"Rachel? Where is she? I want to see her."

I swallowed the knot that came into my throat.

"Grandma," I said. "Rachel died this past winter. Don't you remember?"

"Don't be silly. Your mama was just here visiting me. She came with your daddy. He brought me roses."

My chest felt tight as I looked over at the table beside the bed. There were five light pink roses in a vase. Mama's favorite kind. My neck tingled all the way up into my scalp. Surely Daddy would have no reason to visit Grandma.

"Mama's dead," I said. "Grandpa must have brought the roses."

"Who?"

"Grandpa," I repeated. "Your husband. The man who visited you today."

Grandma frowned and blew a short puff of air through her lips. "He's not my husband. I'd never marry someone that mean."

I sat down hard on the floor. I took her hand in mine and squeezed it. My voice sounded odd when I spoke to her. "Why do you think he's mean?"

"He wouldn't even take me for a drive in his car." Grandma stuck out her lower lip like a little kid. "Said he didn't have one. But I know better." She tapped the side of her head with her finger and grinned like she was telling me some secret.

I smiled. Grandpa was the one without the car, not Daddy.

"He doesn't have a car, really, Grandma. He never got another one after the accident."

"Accident. What accident?"

Before I could answer, a man in a white coat came in with two cans of Coke and two straws.

"Opal said you wanted these," he said.

"Thank you," Grandma said. She took both cans and passed one to me.

"Thanks," I said. I put my Coke on the dresser. "I'll be right back, Grandma."

I walked out of the room and down to the nurses' desk. What sense would it make for Daddy to visit Grandma, of all people? But then, when had Daddy ever made any sense? I guess I just wanted to hear it from Opal. If I did, I'd sleep better that night.

Opal looked up from a chart she was reading at her desk. She raised her eyebrows, waiting for me to say something.

"Was anyone here besides Grandpa and me to visit Grandma today?" I asked.

"Not that I know of," she said. "'Course, somebody could have come in without me seeing them. We get visitors through the side doors all the time." That was not exactly what I wanted to hear. I felt light-headed and put my hand on the wall to steady myself as I walked back.

At Grandma's door I heard funny slurping noises. The gurgling didn't make sense until I got closer. I found Grandma pouring Coke into Birdie's mouth a little at a time. Birdie was drinking it as fast as she could.

I sat down on the floor beside them both and started laughing. Then I started crying.

C H A P T E R

N
I
N
E

Don't cry, little girl," Grandma said. "I didn't give the dog *your* Coke." She handed me the can from the dresser, then sat down beside me on the floor and put her arm around my shoulders. "Now, tell me what that mean man did to you," she said.

I held out my hand to Grandma. She frowned and sucked in her breath.

"That mean man who was here today did this? He can't get away with that. He has to pay. He hurt you. And he hurt me too."

"Daddy hurt me," I said. "Not Grandpa."

"That's what I said. That mean man."

I took Grandpa's picture from the dresser.

"Is this the man who visited you today?" I asked.

"Of course. That's Tom, my husband. He's here all the time."

"Did someone else visit you today?"

"I told you already!" Grandma put her lip out again and got up from the floor. "Why doesn't anybody listen? I'm going to take a shower." She stomped into the bathroom and slammed the door.

"Grandma!" I called after her. "I am listening."

I heard the toilet flush, then heard Grandma singing "We're Off to See the Wizard" at the top of her voice. Could that day get any stranger?

I put Grandpa's picture back next to the roses. Mama roses.

"You okay?"

The sound of Mr. Chitwood's voice made me jump. He was sitting in his wheelchair in the doorway.

"I'm fine. . . ." I said, and swallowed hard to keep from bawling again. "I gotta go home. Tell Grandma good-bye for me, would you? She probably won't even remember I was here."

"Sure she will," Mr. Chitwood said. He patted my arm as I walked past him. I bent over and gave him a hug.

"Do you need anything before I go?" I asked.

"Nothing," he replied. "But when you come again, I sure would love to have a chocolate bar." He grinned.

I smiled back. "What's your favorite?"

He closed his eyes and sighed. "Milky Way."

"I'll bring it as soon as I can," I said.

"You're a saint," Mr. Chitwood exclaimed.

I called to Birdie and we went through the side exit together. I waited outside a few minutes to see if anyone from the front desk would come to check who had opened the door. No one did.

I didn't know what to think about what Grandma had said. It was hard to tell whether she knew what she was talking about or if she dreamed the whole thing up.

Mostly, I didn't want to think about Daddy. I didn't want to wonder if it was him calling when the phone rang, or him driving up the street whenever I heard a car. I didn't want to wonder where he was or what he was doing. Or if he was sorry. I didn't want people to know I had a daddy like that. I just wanted to be rid of Daddy once and for all.

I headed toward town and Grandpa's station to get Mr. Chitwood's candy bar—so I wouldn't forget. While I walked, I started in thinking what I would say to Daddy before I shot him.

For starters, I'd tell him that I hated him. 'Course, he'd probably figure that out when he saw me pointing the gun at him. I'd also tell him that Mama hated him, which I wasn't even sure about—but I knew she would have after what he'd done to me. And I'd remind him how Mama had always treated him so much better than he deserved.

He'd probably cry—he always cried when he was drunk, and drunk was the only way he was anymore. After he sniffled a little, he'd ask me to forgive him and I'd say "No." Just like that. "No." Then he'd start to get mad. That's when I'd kill him. No more talk. No more anything.

I walked faster and faster through the woods to town, pushing through brush that was up to my waist. Stickers clung to my socks, but I kept charging. Pretty soon I was out of breath. Birdie trotted along beside me with her tongue hanging out.

I stopped for a minute and patted her bony head. Then we started walking again more slowly. Birdie sniffed the ground. Every once in a while she held her head up and smelled the air. A squirrel tried a daring leap above our heads, missed the branch, and landed with a plop right beside us. It seemed paralyzed for a moment, then shook its head and ran off through the woods. Birdie barked and scampered into the brush after it.

I called to her, but she ignored me and kept running. In a little while I heard another dog barking in the distance, and it sounded like Birdie was answering it.

So much for the comfort of a dog. I'm not sure what I had expected when I got her. Maybe walks in the woods every morning and going down to the lake to swim together—but lately she always seemed to be off by herself somewhere. I couldn't really blame her for liking to be alone. Since she was a stray, she'd probably spent most of her life on her own, doing whatever she wanted.

When I got to town, I speeded up again and stuck to the busiest streets. If Daddy showed up, I wanted lots of people around. When I got to Grandpa's station, he didn't seem surprised to see me.

"How was your day?" he asked. I'd left him a note about going to the Dairy Deal, and then he'd just happened to walk by there, so he knew I'd been with Dex. Of course, he didn't know about what Grandma had said, and I couldn't bring myself to tell him. I just shrugged in answer to his question.

Grandpa put his arm around my shoulders. "Want to help me work on the Chevy?" He pointed to a truck up on the lift in the garage. "You got to start training for a career soon," he joked.

I smiled and shook my head. "Mr. Chitwood asked me to bring him a Milky Way," I said. Grandpa reached under the counter and brought out a whole box of Milky Ways.

"Think this is enough?" he asked.

I laughed. "That ought to do for a day or so."

"I'm going to give Joy a call and see if she's ready to go home," he said. "She wants us to get barbecue for supper and rent a movie."

Sometimes when I was with Grandpa and Joy, I got the best feeling. It must be the way kids with real families felt all the time. Like they belonged.

For a little while, standing there with Grandpa while he talked on the phone with Joy, I felt better. Daddy seemed further away somehow. Almost like a ghost.

Then I saw a familiar car driving down Main toward me. A maroon LTD with a torn black vinyl top. The blue sky was reflected in the windshield, so I couldn't see the driver. I didn't need to.

CHAPTER

TEN

I had never fainted in my life. Not at Mama's funeral. Not when Daddy did what he did. Maybe I just forgot to breathe. Anyway, I keeled over right there in the Shell station.

When I opened my eyes, Joy was kneeling beside me. Her face was red and sweaty, and her hand shook when she patted my cheek. Grandpa knelt beside her, but he wasn't looking at me. He was looking out the window.

"She's awake, Tom," Joy said.

"There's my girl," Grandpa said. He put a firm hand on my shoulder.

"Lordy, Ellie, you liked to give me a heart attack," Joy said. "I ran all the way over here."

I smiled at the idea of Joy running up Main Street. "Why didn't you drive?" I asked. My voice squeaked like it did sometimes when I was just waking up in the morning.

Joy's mouth dropped open. "Why didn't I drive, Tom?" she asked Grandpa.

He shrugged his shoulders and smiled down at me. "I have no idea."

Joy laughed and patted my cheek again. "See how rattled you got me?"

"You okay?" Grandpa asked.

"I think so," I said. My heart beat faster as I remembered the car coming down Main Street. Daddy's car. But I couldn't tell Grandpa. He'd call the police. That would spoil the plan.

"I must have gotten too hot on the way over," I finally said. I started to get up.

"Slowly, now," Grandpa said.

"Think we best take her over to Konowa to have her checked out?" Joy asked.

"I don't know," Grandpa said. Again he looked out

the window. I swear it was a full minute before he turned back to us. "Why don't we just take her home, make her eat barbecue and sit under the fan. I think she'll be okay."

He winked at me and I smiled. My legs felt wobbly when I stood up, but I don't think anybody noticed. I sat in Grandpa's desk chair while Joy went to get her car and Grandpa washed his hands.

Lots of cars drove past. I wondered if I had imagined the whole thing. Maybe I had wanted Daddy to be there. Wanted to get it over with.

The next day was rainy. Joy and Grandpa had planned a big fishing trip with their friends but decided to cancel. A little rain had never stopped them from going before, so I figured they were still worried about me.

When the doorbell rang that afternoon, I almost jumped out of my skin. Grandpa went to the door.

"Hi, Mr. Whiteday," I heard Dex say. "Is Ellie here?"

Grandpa told him I was and opened the door to let him in. Dex closed the umbrella he was carrying and leaned it next to the door. He didn't have on his cap, and his blond hair looked like it'd just been washed. Grandpa sat back down in his recliner and pretended to look at the TV.

Dex sat on the couch beside me. He cleared his throat like he was nervous or something. To tell you the truth, I was too. I really liked Dex. And it seemed as though he somehow liked me too. But he hadn't asked about my hand, and I wondered how long it would take before he did.

"You want to go to the Dairy Deal or something?" he asked suddenly. If he was going to ask me questions, I sure didn't want to be around a bunch of other kids when he did.

"We could go to the nursing home," I said.

"What?"

"I promised to bring my friend Mr. Chitwood a candy bar," I said. "Grandpa gave me a whole box of Milky Ways."

"Hey, I know him too," Dex said. "He gave my dad his first job. He's a nice old guy. I like visiting him."

I looked at Grandpa then. He was grinning but not looking my way. "Get an umbrella," he said. "And if it starts thundering, you stay put. I'll send Joy to get you."

I pulled on my sneakers and grabbed the box of Milky Ways. I called Birdie and we tramped out into the muck.

Dex didn't say anything as we walked up the street. When we passed his house, his dog, Jake, bounded off the porch. Jake and Birdie splashed around each other in the mud, then ran off together.

"Birdie!" I yelled.

"What's wrong?" Dex asked.

"My dog never sticks with me when we go out."

"Some dogs are like that," Dex said.

I nodded. "Seems like she's never around when I want her for a walk. When she does go with me, she runs off. You'd think a pregnant dog would stick closer to home."

"Bet you didn't know she's started coming to get Jake every morning, did you?" Dex asked with a grin.

I shook my head and splashed into a puddle that was deeper than I expected. The cool water seeped into my shoes.

"Every morning when you let Birdie out, she runs up here," Dex explained. "If Jake's not out, she just lies down on the porch and waits. When we let him out, off they go into the woods. Hunting, I guess."

I don't know why this bothered me so much. Birdie was just being a regular dog. It was probably normal for her to like another dog better than me.

We tramped along in silence for a few minutes— except for the squishing sound of my shoes. We turned right on Seminole and went down the middle of the paved street. I didn't like it, but I couldn't think of any good reason to explain to Dex why I wanted to walk through the woods on the side of the road instead.

"Do you visit Mr. Chitwood often?" Dex asked.

"I see Grandma a couple of times a week," I said. "I usually drop by to see Mr. Chitwood too. Do you come to see him often?"

"I visit him whenever Dad goes—which used to be once a month. But Dad's been pretty busy lately. We haven't been since April."

"What's your dad do?" I asked.

"You don't know?"

"Should I?"

"If you live in Drasco you should," Dex said. He grinned at me. I wondered what was so funny. "Dad's the head cop."

"Your dad's the chief of police?" I asked, and tried not to look too surprised. Dex must have known about my hand when he first met me. The cops back home had said they'd make sure that Drasco cops were sent everything they had on Daddy. Unless Dex's dad was really closemouthed, he'd have told his wife and kids. Great.

Dex laughed. "Dad's got one whole other police officer to boss around too. He's Dad's cousin Dwayne. But Dad says it beats Tulsa, where he used to work."

I had seen Drasco's one-room jailhouse. There was a cell off to the side, two desks, a computer, and a telephone. That was about it. I'd met Dwayne when I first moved there, but the chief had been home sick with the flu. Grandpa never bothered to tell me that he lived down the street—or that he was Dex's dad.

Just as we got to the nursing home driveway, our dogs came running out of the woods, stopped, and shook water all over us.

"Hey!" I said, wiping my face with the sleeve of my T-shirt. Dex laughed and opened and closed his umbrella at Jake, getting him back. Jake ran a few feet away and barked. Birdie sat down and put her paw out like she was apologizing. I shook it and patted her head.

When we got inside the nursing home, Mr. Chitwood was waiting by the front desk.

"The most beautiful girl that ever walked the earth," he said when he saw me. I felt my face get hot. "Your grandpa called to tell me you were on your way here with your boyfriend." He smiled real wide, showing his bright false teeth. My ears were definitely on fire now. I didn't dare look at Dex. Mr. Chitwood went on. "He said you had something special for me?"

I handed him the box of Milky Ways. Mr. Chitwood frowned as he looked at the box.

"What?" I asked. "That's the kind you said you wanted, isn't it?"

"Shoot. I thought you were going to give me a hug."

I laughed, bent down, and hugged him. He patted my back with his frail hands, then smiled at the box in his lap.

"Boy, this is going to make me popular with the ladies. . . ."

"Chocolate gets 'em every time, doesn't it?" Dex said, and gave Mr. Chitwood the thumbs-up sign.

"Push me into that room, Dexter, and watch this."

Dexter did as he was told. I stayed in the hall.

"Estelle? Look what I brung you."

"If you aren't the sweetest man," a weak voice said.

Dex turned around and grinned at me. I smiled back and hoped I wasn't going to get red-faced again.

"I'm going to go say hi to Grandma," I said. Dex nodded.

I hurried down to the far end of the hall. It was always kind of strange going to see her, never knowing if she would be "in," so to speak.

Grandma was sitting in a chair staring out the window as usual. When I walked up beside her, she looked at me. A good sign.

"That mean man was here again today," she said.

I couldn't believe she would remember what we talked about last time. The roses on her dresser, a little wilted now, were the same ones from the day before at least.

"The mean man?" I asked. "You mean Grandpa?" I thought maybe Grandpa had come up to see her that morning while I was still asleep.

"He said he was sorry," she went on. "But I don't believe him. I don't think he's sorry about anything. He said he'd tell you himself. I told him he'd better not."

"Sorry about the car accident? Sorry for what happened to you?"

Grandma's eyes met mine and didn't look away. She was *in*. No question about it.

"He said he was sorry about what he did to *you*," she said slowly.

I couldn't breathe. My chest felt tight and my hands started to shake. Grandma's room was too dark and small. So I ran.

CHAPTER

ELEVEN

Get away. That's all I could think of when I started running. Someone called my name as I flung open the side door of the nursing home and felt the rain on my face. Daddy, I thought. Daddy's after me. Get Grandpa's gun. Run.

I sprinted into the trees and bushes on the other side of the nursing home driveway. Everything was a blur of green and brown. I heard splashing behind me and my name being called.

"Ellie!"

Saplings and brush pulled at me; mud sucked at my

feet. I couldn't run nearly as fast as I needed to. And I didn't dare turn around. But Daddy was there. I could hear his footsteps. I felt him closing in on me.

Then I tripped. It happened so fast that the breath was knocked out of me. I lay on my side. Couldn't breathe, couldn't scream, couldn't move. And Daddy was still coming. I could see his shadowy figure running through the trees toward me.

"Ellie!" he called.

Suddenly Birdie was beside me licking my face. I pulled in a great gulp of air and looked up. Daddy was standing over me now. A dark figure looking down. He didn't say anything. I sat up and scooted backward to get away.

"Ellie," he said in a soft voice. Then he put out his hand and touched my arm. The scream that had been waiting inside of me flew out. I yelled long and hard and longer still. I covered my ears to drown out the noise.

He shook me. Birdie barked. And I stopped. I gulped for air again and looked at the person kneeling in front of me holding on to my arms.

"Ellie?" Dex said. "Ellie." Then he sat down beside me. Birdie laid her head in my lap. I put my left hand on Birdie, stroked her wet fur, and tried to breathe like a normal person.

"I thought you were Daddy," I finally said.

"I know. It's okay. He's not here."

I nodded.

Dex reached out to pet Birdie too, and ended up bumping my hand. My hand with the stubby fingers. I knew he was looking at them.

"Daddy did that to me."

"I know."

Daddy had made me play cards every day after school. Even the day of Mama's funeral. I didn't know why. Maybe he thought it would make him feel better. It was okay when he wasn't drinking. But when he was, he'd make me play for money, and have a fit if he lost. I shivered, remembering.

I kept petting Birdie and so did Dex. I tried to breathe deep and stop shaking while I remembered. I had come home one day and Daddy was sitting there in his underwear with a bottle of Jack Daniel's. He was slicing himself some cheese with his hunting knife. He didn't say anything, just pointed that shiny knife at the chair and the cards he'd already dealt out for me.

"I told Daddy I wouldn't play cards with him," I said.

Dex patted my arm and then went back to petting Birdie. He didn't look at me, but I knew he was waiting for me to say more. I swallowed.

Daddy's face had turned red, like he was boiling inside. When he finally spoke, he sounded like a hissing snake.

"Daddy told me to SIT. Just like that—SIT. As if I were a dog."

"What did you do?" Dex asked.

"I put my hands on the table and leaned forward to look right into his eyes. I'd had enough. Then I just said 'No,' as loud as you please."

"Did he say anything?"

"Not a word. He just looked like he couldn't quite believe I'd cross him like that. So I leaned even closer and said it again. 'No.'"

"From what I've heard about your daddy, that was pretty brave."

"Or stupid," I said. "When he raised up that knife, it seemed like he did it so slowly that surely I could have moved out of the way. But I didn't. Then WHACK! My fingers were lying there on the table."

"God, Ellie," Dex said.

"Funny. That's what Daddy said. He acted right nice, soon as he saw all the blood."

There had been so much blood. That's all I kept thinking. Nobody could bleed that much and hurt that much and still live. I think I was hoping I was gonna die.

"Did he take you to the hospital?" Dex asked.

I nodded. "Wrapped my hand up in his undershirt and drove me twenty miles to Tulsa. Then ran off. The nurse told him if he brought my fingers, maybe they could put them back on. He promised he'd get them. But he never came back."

I looked down at my hand for a minute—the pink stubs that ended just above my knuckles. They were all wet now from the rain that was still barely sprinkling. I tried to remember what my hand had looked like before.

"Did the hospital call your grandpa?"

I nodded. "It took a while. At first I told the doctor it was an accident. But she didn't believe me. Then when Daddy didn't come back, I told her the truth, and she had the nurse call Grandpa."

"What'd your grandpa say?"

"Not much. He just hugged me and said he'd take me home with him."

I thought back to that day and how Joy was there and how she cried a lot. The doctor made me stay in the hospital overnight, and Grandpa and Joy stayed right there with me, sleeping in chairs. The doctor gave me some pain pills, so I slept a lot.

"When I was in the hospital, I woke up once and heard Joy saying how concerned she was about me. But she didn't need to worry. I'm okay now."

"'Course you are," Dex said.

I sighed and wiped my face with the arm of my wet T-shirt.

"You're the first person I've told since the doctor."

Dex didn't answer, just coughed a nervous cough—like he didn't know what to say. Birdie lifted her head from my lap and licked my face.

Dex stood up and helped me up beside him. "Did your dad tell you all about me?"

"A little," Dex said. "Said your daddy was wanted."

"Did he tell you to come over and meet me too?"

"No," he answered. I could tell by the slow way he said the word that it wasn't the truth.

"Liar."

"Dad didn't, honest," he said. "But Mom did. She said you were nice and needed a friend."

I closed my eyes to keep the tears inside. It didn't work. I started walking, fast.

"Now don't run away, Ellie," Dex said. He grabbed my arm to slow me down. "I came to say hello 'cause Mom told me to, but I came back because I liked you. We had fun the other day. Didn't we?"

I nodded, afraid to speak just yet. Finally I found my voice. "Why didn't you ask about my fingers when you saw them the first time?"

"I already knew about them, for starters," he said. "And I didn't figure it was something you'd want to talk about. It's just something I should know about you if we're friends. Like me not being able to read so good. But we don't have to talk it to death."

I felt so relieved that he understood, I started crying again. I know it didn't make sense.

Dex put his hand on my shoulder and looked down at me. "Ellie, you have got to quit crying before we get home, or your grandpa is going to kill me first and ask questions later. You know how he is." His smile made me laugh.

I knew what he meant. Grandpa didn't exactly have a reputation for being easygoing.

We hiked through the trees now with our dogs just ahead of us. I didn't make any move to walk out on the road, and Dex didn't either.

"Now, what made you think I was your daddy back there?" he asked.

I shrugged. "I think I just went crazy for a few minutes."

Dex didn't ask any more questions. I was glad. I'd probably tell him someday about what Grandma said, but I reckoned both of us were sick of talk right then. The rest of the way we walked in silence except for a rumble of thunder that was getting closer. We reached Grandpa's porch just as lightning and thunder crackled and boomed overhead. Birdie whined beside me, anxious to get inside.

At the door Dex said, "You okay?"

I nodded, afraid I might start crying again.

"I'll call you later," he said, then ran up the street to his house. I stood on the porch for a minute watching him go, glad to have a friend who understood.

CHAPTER

TWELVE

Inside, I found Grandpa standing in the kitchen doorway talking on the phone. The long white cord coiled behind him back into the kitchen. When he saw me, he frowned. Thunder rumbled again, as if he'd willed it.

"Never mind, Joy," he said into the phone. "She just walked in."

"Sorry," I told him. "We started home before the thunder."

He smiled a little and handed me a towel from the laundry basket on the kitchen table. "Get on dry clothes," he said. "I'll make some supper. We're just having sandwiches tonight."

I hung my wet clothes over the tub and put on jeans and a T-shirt. I wrapped my hair in the towel and walked back to the kitchen. While Grandpa spread tuna salad on bread, I sat down at the table and dealt myself a hand of solitaire. I didn't bother to shuffle.

Though I wasn't really interested, it was comforting to have the cards in my hands and see the familiar rows and patterns. My mind was still racing. Grandma. Daddy. Dex. They all kept zipping around inside my head.

"He said he was sorry about what he did to you," Grandma had said. And she *had* been in her right mind when she said it. Why couldn't he stay gone?

My thoughts skipped back to Dex and I smiled, remembering what he had said about my fingers. "It's just something I should know about you if we're friends."

Grandpa put a Coke and a sandwich in front of me. When I looked up at him, he smiled.

"Good day?" he asked.

The question made me start to think about Daddy again. I looked down at the solitaire game I had just lost and started pushing the cards together into a pile.

"Dex . . ." I said out loud, trying to focus again. I felt my face get hot, and looked up at Grandpa. He was still smiling.

"I see," he said.

"You don't either see," I snapped back. I had never, ever spoken to Grandpa like that. I wondered what he'd do. But he just kept grinning and sat down across from me and took a bite of his sandwich.

Every time I looked at him, he was still smiling. Finally I quit looking. When I was finished eating, Grandpa put an ice-cream sandwich on the table in front of me, already unwrapped. I usually hated when he did that, but I ate it anyway in about three gulps and didn't complain.

Grandpa had his hands in soapy water when the phone rang, so I had to answer it.

"Hello," I said. I heard labored breathing and what sounded like someone adjusting the phone on the other end.

"So you made it home okay?" Mr. Chitwood finally said.

I realized then I'd been holding my breath, and let it out.

"Yeah," I said.

"Glad to hear it." He paused. "You know, your

grandma's been telling all sorts of tales lately. I was going to tell you some, but you left before I got the chance."

"Like what?" I asked.

"Well, yesterday she told us she was Senator Boren's wife," he said.

"I guess someone forgot to tell her he's not a senator anymore."

"And the day before, she told us she was a Secret Service agent for the president. Said she'll be guarding him next time he's in the state."

"Seems she has a thing for politicians," I said. Grandpa looked over at me and raised an eyebrow, wondering who I was talking to.

"Listen, Ellie. I don't know what she said to you, but the thing is," Mr. Chitwood said, and then cleared his throat. "She lives in her own world. She doesn't know what's real and what's not. So don't let her upset you. Okay?"

My throat felt tight. Sympathy from other people always did that to me.

"Okay," I finally said, and hung up the phone. Grandpa didn't ask who it was.

Even though I knew what Mr. Chitwood said was true for the most part, I still found myself sticking pretty close to home—and Grandpa's gun. Dex came over almost every day. We didn't talk all that much— just played solitaire sitting side by side on the living room floor. Sometimes we listened to the CDs he brought over. Other times we watched old movies or soap operas.

I tried to make Birdie stay home with me, but she whined so much, I usually gave up and let her out. Her belly was huge now, and I didn't like her going very far from home, but she seemed determined to be off on her own. The only time she stayed with me was when the weather was bad.

It was weird how the more I stayed at home, the more I *wanted* to stay home. Pretty soon just the thought of going outside gave me the shakes. I reckon it was a case of Daddy winning again, even though he wasn't there. He might as well have been. I was too scared even to sit on the porch.

Joy and Grandpa tried to get me to go to the movies in Konowa a few times, but I wouldn't. Dex and his mom invited me to the Philbrook Museum in Tulsa. Mama and I used to love it there. But Daddy knew that, and he could be anywhere.

Then came the day Birdie didn't come home for supper. She'd done that before, and at first I wasn't too worried. Come morning she was always on the back porch sitting right beside the door, waiting to be let in.

But the next day when it was thundering and lightning again and I saw the empty porch, I knew something must be wrong. Birdie hated nothing worse than being out in wild weather. Grandpa said not to worry, she'd turn up. But after he left for work, I phoned Dex.

"Is Birdie at your house?" I asked.

"I don't think so. Jake's right here. I'll check outside."

I heard him set the phone down and walk across the hardwood floor. The screen door squeaked and then his footsteps came back.

"I don't see her," he said. "She been gone long?"

"She didn't come back for supper last night," I said. "And she hates this kind of weather."

"She was a stray. Maybe she knows a place to go when she's too far to make it home."

"But what if she's having those puppies?" I was trying to sound calm, but my voice sounded high-pitched and crazy. "The vet said she was kind of young to give birth. I don't want her to have the puppies by herself."

"I'll help you look for her," Dex offered. "You want to go now or wait for the rain to let up?"

"Now—and thanks," I said, and hung up. I knew that Grandpa wouldn't like my going out in the storm, but this was an emergency.

I got Grandpa's big raincoat from the closet and put on my sneakers by the front door. But before I turned the handle to go outside, I stopped and walked over to the side table next to the recliner. I opened the drawer and took out the gun. I took the bullets from the closet, loaded them into the chamber, and put the gun into the raincoat pocket. The gun bumped against my leg as I headed to Dex's house.

CHAPTER

THIRTEEN

During the weeks I had stayed at home, I had thought about Dex a lot—even when he was right there in the living room with me. I had gone from being glad to have a friend to feeling a bit embarrassed. Acting like a crazy person and telling him all about Daddy changed everything. I sometimes felt self-conscious talking to him. I didn't always know what to say anymore. I had thought about that day at the nursing home so much—talking to Grandma, the crazy run through the trees, sitting in the rain telling Dex everything—that it almost seemed like it had happened to some other Ellie.

Being worried about my dog took my mind off all that. I couldn't stand the idea of Birdie maybe needing me and me not being there. She knew how to take care of herself, but she didn't know about having puppies.

Before I was even halfway up the walk to Dex's front door, he and Jake came out of the house.

"You want to start at the boat landing?" he asked.

I nodded. Birdie liked to go swimming there, and I knew there was an old beat-up wooden boat turned upside down next to the ramp. A scared dog might find a way to get under it.

Dex and I didn't say much as we walked. Jake ran on ahead of us. Thunder crashed overhead, and I could feel Dex looking at me every once in a while, but I didn't look back.

There was no sign of Birdie at the boat landing. No paw prints, no anything. Even though it was only the first place we'd looked, I felt beaten. If Dex hadn't been with me, I think I would have just gone home and gone to bed.

"Let's go over to the nursing home," Dex said. "She might have gone visiting without you. You know how much they like her over there."

We trudged off up the road. Lightning crackled and the rain started coming down in sheets. Dex pointed to the trees.

"Probably drier under there," he said.

We moved into the woods, but it didn't make much difference. Still, I was glad to be there instead of the middle of the road. I had trouble swallowing, and the rain came near to choking me as I panted and breathed it in. We pushed through sticker bushes and maple saplings.

"Hey, slow down," Dex said. He put his hand on my shoulder. I made myself breathe deep and matched my pace to his.

No one at the nursing home had seen Birdie. Mr. Chitwood said he'd seen her with Jake early that morning—or was it the morning before? He couldn't be sure. He said he'd call if she turned up. Grandma wasn't in a talking mood, so I didn't get anything out of her. Opal said she'd keep a lookout.

I felt even more worried after talking to all those people, but Dex kept things going.

"Let's run by your grandpa's station and Joy's shop and the Dairy Deal," he said.

"Grandpa or Joy would have called me if she had shown up," I said.

"Maybe. But let's check anyway," he said. He smiled at me. He was too cheerful for someone who was looking for a dog in a blinding rainstorm.

Grandpa's Back in Thirty Minutes sign was up in the station window, and the same thing was up in Joy's shop. I figured they must have gone for coffee together, but we didn't see them at the diner.

Birdie wasn't at the Dairy Deal either. Ruth said she'd been coming around more lately, but not in the last couple of days. I almost slugged Dex when he asked if I wanted a milk shake or something. How could he think I'd want to eat at such a time?

"No," I said, and glared at him, but it didn't stop him from ordering a cheeseburger, fries, and a chocolate shake—to go. And I did eat some of his salty fries while we walked back to my house in the drizzle. Still, I was exhausted, and mad at Dex and his stupid dog and my stupid dog, wherever she was.

It had stopped raining completely by the time we got to my porch. I didn't bother to ask Dex if he wanted to come in.

"Thanks for helping me look," I said, although I knew I didn't sound very grateful.

"She'll come home soon," he answered. I didn't look back at him as I went inside and closed the door.

The house smelled like toast and coffee, as if Grandpa and Joy had been back for a snack. Before I had a chance to take off Grandpa's raincoat, the phone rang. I raced to grab it, hoping it was news about Birdie. I heard a familiar fumbling with the phone on the other end.

"Ellie?" Mr. Chitwood's voice sounded far away, like he hadn't quite gotten the phone next to his mouth yet.

"This is me," I said. "Did you find Birdie?"

"Your daddy," said Mr. Chitwood, louder now, and he was talking faster than he'd probably ever talked in his life. "Your daddy was here, Ellie. I haven't seen him in a long time, but I'm sure it was him. I told Opal to call the chief and your grandpa. What?" Mr. Chitwood was talking to someone in the room with him. "Damnation," he said, coming back on the line. "Ellie, your grandma's gone missing too. Opal said there's no answer at Joy's shop or at the gas station, but she'll keep trying. The chief's out with Dwayne somewhere too, but his wife is calling him in the car. Don't know if your daddy's on his way to see you. So you just lock the doors and stay inside, you hear?"

I didn't answer. I couldn't. I was too busy thinking faster than Mr. Chitwood was talking. Inside the raincoat pocket the gun felt cool and heavy. I slipped my hand around the grip without putting my finger on the trigger.

"Ellie?" Mr. Chitwood asked. "You okay?"

"Yeah," I said. Then I hung up the phone, pushed open the door, and went out onto the front porch to wait.

CHAPTER

FOURTEEN

I sat down on the top step of the porch. The clouds were moving on, and the air was hotter and thicker. I took off the raincoat, reached into the pocket, and took out the gun. It was a revolver. The kind that cowboys use to shoot bad guys.

The metal of the gun felt warm now from the heat of my hand. I held it in my right hand and stuck my arm out straight in front of me. Then I put my stubby fingers on the gun too. Holding my breath, I aimed at the tree across the street. I was glad that I remembered how to shoot.

I kept hold of the gun but let it rest on my lap. I ran my index finger down the barrel of the revolver and imagined the sound of the bullet coming from inside. It would be loud. Heard all over Drasco, probably.

Birds chirped around me. They were happy that the storm was over. I remembered a time when Mama and I had listened to the birds. We had talked about getting a tape and learning which birds sang what songs. But we never did. It was just talk. Just like the talk about her leaving Daddy. Talking always seemed to take the energy out of an idea for her. For me too. Maybe that's why I hadn't told anyone about my plan for Daddy.

I really didn't feel scared sitting on the steps waiting. It was sort of like the feeling I had when Mama died. I had dreaded going to her funeral and walked around shaking and crying the three days before. But when it was finally time, I sat in the church and calmly listened to Pastor Lyons preach about Mama just the same as if I were at a regular Sunday sermon.

When I heard gravel crunching under the tires of a car in the driveway, I didn't look up right away. I knew who it was.

The car door opened—screeking like it always had. When the door slammed I looked up, and there was Daddy standing beside the maroon LTD, looking back at me. He had on a plaid shirt and Levi's that were dirty and too big for him. His eyes looked red and he hadn't shaved in days.

"Hey, Ellie," he finally said. He stuck his hands in his pockets and fell back against the car. Drunk. I didn't think he'd noticed the gun just yet.

"Why did you have to come here?" I asked.

"I had to talk to you," he said. "I would have talked to you on the phone—but you hung up on me."

"I don't want you here," I said.

"Listen," he said. "Please?"

I stared at him for minute and then shifted my gaze to the gun in my lap.

"I just wanted to say . . ." he started, then stopped to clear his throat. He tried to stand up straighter without the help of the car, but stumbled back. "I just wanted to say I'm really, truly sorry for what I done to you. I was drunk, Ellie. I didn't know what I was doing."

"You're always drunk. You never know what you're doing. Just like now."

I looked straight at him and didn't turn away as he looked back at me and then down at the ground. I was still staring at him when he looked up again.

"You don't believe me?" he asked. "I really *am* sorry."

"Sorry for what?" I yelled.

"Sorry for hurting you."

"Say it! Say what you're sorry for!"

Tears welled up in my eyes, and my throat felt like it was closing. I willed myself not to cry.

I could see him swallow. He closed his eyes and ran his hands through his hair. His shoulders rose and fell as he took a deep breath.

"I'm sorry for cutting off your fingers," he said softly.

"What? I can't hear you."

"I'm sorry for cutting off your fingers. Ellie, please," he whined. "You're my daughter. I miss your mama and I miss you. I love you."

I laughed. I hadn't meant to, but Daddy's lines sounded like he had practiced what he thought was the right thing to say to me.

"Ellie, please," he whined again. "We can still be a family. You and me."

I stopped laughing then. How could he even think that was possible?

"Mama and me were a family. You were never part of it," I said.

He winced as if I'd slapped him. Then he narrowed his eyes, pushed himself away from the car, and started to weave toward me. I picked up the gun from my lap and pointed it straight at his head. He stopped and squinted at me. It must've taken him a second or two to focus. When he finally did, his mouth dropped open.

"Ellie?" he asked. "What are you doing?"

"Getting you out of my life. I just wish I'd had the nerve to do it when Mama was alive."

"I'm your daddy. You can't shoot me."

"I'm through being afraid." I pulled the hammer back on the revolver, and it made a soft click. Daddy's eyes widened but his voice got sweet and syrupy.

"You won't shoot me. You know you won't. Okay, I wasn't a good daddy, but you won't shoot me. You're too nice a person. You don't have it in you any more than your mama did. You *can't* shoot me."

"No. But I sure as hell can!" It was Grandpa. He was standing by the corner of our house, holding a shotgun that looked about as big as me. "Get inside, Ellie."

"No." I kept the revolver aimed at Daddy. "I want him out of my life."

"I wouldn't mind if you shot him. But trust me, honey. Killing him won't get him out of your life. It will just keep him with you forever."

"Listen to your grandpa," Daddy said. He started to walk toward me again. Grandpa pumped the shotgun. The sound sliced through the air with the loud clicking of metal against metal. Daddy dropped to his knees on the grass about three feet in front of me, but kept looking right at me.

"Don't think for a minute that my advice to Ellie will stop *me* from shooting you," Grandpa said.

"Police are on their way," Joy said from her porch. "If you shoot him, Tom, I won't visit you while you rot in McAlister."

"Thanks," Grandpa said.

"I just came to apologize," Daddy said. "Why do you all want to kill me?" He looked at me when he said it.

I realized he could still amaze me. Couldn't he see what he'd done to me and Mama? Long before he used his knife on me, he'd been cutting away at our lives. I carefully put the hammer back down on the revolver and walked the few steps over to him, the gun dangling at my side. I looked down at him, and he smiled a silly grin up at me. I smelled stale whiskey on his breath.

"I hate you," I said. "I never want to see you again. Ever. And when you die, I know you'll burn in hell."

The smile on Daddy's face faded. I knew before he even raised his hand that he was going to slap me.

But suddenly there was a scream like a panther, and a blur of long dark hair and pale skin whizzed in front of me and knocked Daddy to the ground. Grandma.

CHAPTER

FIFTEEN

Everything happened real fast after that. Grandma's hands gripped Daddy's neck like a vise. She sat on his chest, pinning his arms to his sides. He tried to kick her off, but he was drunk and no match for Grandma's kind of anger and craziness. His eyes rolled back in his head and I could hear him gagging.

"Marie!" Joy screamed, and came running. The screen door slammed behind her. Grandpa laid down his shotgun and ran to Grandma too.

"Marie," Grandpa said, trying to free Grandma's hands. "You can let go now, honey. It'll be okay."

Grandma relaxed her grip some, but she didn't move until Dex's dad, Mr. Hill, drove up and jumped out of his police car.

Mr. Hill rolled Daddy over, handcuffed him and read him his rights while he lay facedown on the ground. I couldn't tell if he was breathing.

A few seconds later Dex ran down the street with Jake.

"You okay?" he asked. I think I nodded back. Mostly I just stood there watching and listening to all the commotion—like it was some strange show on TV.

Grandma sat on the porch glaring at Daddy while Joy and Grandpa held her hands on either side. Her breathing was heavy and loud, and her hair hung in long black straggles over her face. Grandpa reached up and gently pushed her hair out of her eyes. I understood now about the toast and coffee inside. Grandma had decided to make us dinner.

Mr. Hill's cousin Dwayne drove up in the other Drasco City police car and got out.

"Man," he said. "Looks like I missed all the excitement."

"Shut up, Dwayne," Mr. Hill said. "Take this fugitive here down to the station. Call over to Tulsa County. They're just dying to have a little chat with him."

Dwayne nodded and gave me a thumbs-up sign. I tried to smile but couldn't quite manage it. Daddy got up with Dwayne's help and walked to the police car. Just before he got in, Daddy bent forward and threw up all over the grass. When he was finished, Dwayne put him in the back of the cruiser.

"You better not be doing that in my car," Dwayne said. "I'll make you clean it up."

Daddy didn't say anything, just leaned back in the seat while Dwayne closed the door. I walked over to the car and looked in the window. He flinched but didn't look at me. Dwayne got in and drove off. I watched the car all the way down the road, expecting something—I don't know what—to happen.

We all ended up in the kitchen next. Mr. Hill wrote in his notebook and asked us a bunch of questions. Grandma muttered something about putting dinner on the table and about stopping that mean man, but then she clammed up and wouldn't say anything else.

"So, Mr. Chitwood is the one who called you?" Mr. Hill looked at me.

I nodded.

"He left us messages too," Grandpa said, motioning to Joy.

"We went and picked up some coffee and then stopped by my house to get some cake," Joy said. "That's when we heard the message."

"Guess I'll make a run over to see Mr. Chitwood later and get his statement," Mr. Hill said. He wrote something in his book. "Got any good reasons why Ellie's daddy would go talk to Marie? Especially in her condition?"

It was a good question, but I didn't really care about the answer. Daddy was a drunk—when did he ever need a reason other than that?

"The only thing I can figure is that Marie used to have a soft spot for Vince," Grandpa said. He tipped his chair back on two legs and put his hands in his pockets. He looked at Grandma. "She always tried to see his point of view. It got her and Rachel into more than a few knock-down-drag-outs, I can tell you."

Grandma sat with her hands in her lap, staring down at the table. Her shoulders started to shake and I could see tears slide down her cheeks. Grandpa put an arm around her and she laid her head on his shoulder. I'd never known about Grandma and Daddy. I couldn't quite believe it.

"Obviously she changed her mind about him," Mr. Hill said without smiling.

"Obviously," Grandpa said.

I didn't want to sit there anymore going over why Daddy was Daddy and who knew what. I got up and went into the bathroom and locked the door. I grabbed a handful of tissues and sat down on the edge of the tub. I didn't know I had gone in there to cry, but that's what happened.

I started thinking about Mama and how much I wanted her to be there, and the tears just flowed. Then I remembered that Birdie was still gone too, and I felt even worse. I thought about how Grandpa had been ready to kill Daddy, and Grandma almost did. And I cried even harder. It didn't make any sense to me to be crying then, when it was all over, and I tried to stop, but I just couldn't.

I tried to cry quietly. I didn't want a scene. I figured everyone'd had just about enough of that sort of thing for one day. I kept wadding up handfuls of tissue in front of my face and listening to the murmur of voices out in the kitchen. Finally, when I thought I had control of myself, I looked in the mirror and almost started crying all over again. There was no way everyone wouldn't know from looking at me exactly what I'd been doing.

I ran cold water in the sink and splashed it on my face. It calmed me down some, but it didn't make me look any better.

While I stood there wondering how long it would be before my eyes stopped looking red and puffy, I heard a yip. It wasn't the kind of sound that Birdie would make. But it *was* a doggy kind of sound. I stooped down and listened closely. I heard more yips. They were coming from under the house.

I threw open the bathroom door and ran outside.

"Ellie!" Grandpa called after me. I heard a chair clunk on the kitchen floor, then voices and footsteps behind me. I didn't stop to hear what anyone was saying. I ran to the side of the house to the hole in the crawl space. The same place the cats had gotten in that night. I stuck my head through the hole.

"Birdie!" I called.

I heard a heavy groan and another couple of yips. As my eyes adjusted to the dim light, I could see Birdie's bulky form lying against the far wall. She was panting and three puppies were whining beside her.

"Birdie," I whispered. She didn't seem to hear me. She was too busy. While I watched, she panted and struggled and out popped one last puppy. "Good girl," I said when I finally found my voice. This time she heard me and wagged her tail weakly. When I turned around, Grandpa and Joy and Dex and his dad and even Grandma were looking at me, smiling.

"I found Birdie," I said. "And her four puppies."

"Let me see," Dex said, and stuck his head into the hole. After a few minutes he stuck his head back out long enough to rip off another board, then wiggled his whole body under the house.

"I want to make sure the puppies are okay," he yelled back to me.

I watched as he petted Birdie and made soft clicking noises to the puppies.

In a few minutes he worked his way back and passed me something warm and squirmy wrapped in his OSU baseball cap. I pulled it into the sunshine before I took a look.

"I think this makes us related or something," he said. He climbed out of the hole and sat beside me on the ground.

I opened the cap and saw a wet, pudgy little puppy shaped in every way like Birdie but with Jake's white chest, brown ears, and black body. There was no doubt who the father was.

"Cute, huh?" Dex said.

The puppy looked so sweet, I was afraid I was going to cry again. I just nodded and smiled.

Everyone admired the puppy for a few minutes; then Dex crawled back under the house and put it back with its family. Grandpa and Joy left to drive Grandma back to the nursing home, and Dex's dad went to check on his prisoner. That left me and Dex sitting on the front porch steps alone, with Jake lying nearby in the grass.

Dex and I didn't talk much. He said he was glad Daddy was caught, and I said I was too. He said he was glad I'd found Birdie, and I said I was too. I think Dex was pretty happy when Grandpa and Joy drove up and walked past us into the house.

"I guess I'd better be getting home now," he said.

"You want to get together tomorrow?" I asked.

"Sure," he said. He seemed surprised. Heck, I surprised myself. "I'll come over after lunch—as long as we don't have to play any more solitaire."

I laughed. "I'm pretty sick of solitaire myself. Maybe we can go swimming or something."

"Good," he said. Then he kissed me and ran off up the street.